MEET THE KEY WORKERS

TRANSPORTATION WORKERS

BY
SHALINI VALLEPUR

KidHaven
PUBLISHING

Published in 2024 by
KidHaven Publishing, an Imprint of Greenhaven Publishing, LLC
2544 Clinton St., Buffalo, NY 14224

Written by: Shalini Vallepur
Edited by: John Wood
Designed by: Jasmine Pointer

Cataloging-in-Publication Data

Names: Vallepur, Shalini.
Title: Transportation workers / Shalini Vallepur.
Description: New York : KidHaven Publishing, 2024. | Series: Meet the key workers | Includes glossary and index.
Identifiers: ISBN 9781534544543 (pbk) | ISBN 9781534544550 (library bound) | ISBN 9781534544567 (ebook)
Subjects: LCSH: Occupation-- Juvenile literature | Trasportation-- Juvenile literature
Classification: LCC HD8039.T7 V35 2024 | DDC 388.092--dc24

Manufactured in the United States of America

CPSIA compliance information: Batch #CSKH24: For further information contact Greenhaven Publishing LLC at 1-844-317-7404.

Please visit our website, www.greenhavenpublishing.com. For a free color catalog of all our high-quality books, call toll free 1-844-317-7404 or fax 1-844-317-7405.

Find us on

Image Credits

All images are courtesy of Shutterstock.com, unless otherwise specified. With thanks to Getty Images, Thinkstock Photo and iStockphoto.

Cover – MonkeyBusinessImages, SIVStockStudio, Dzm1try, LineTale, NWM, vladwel, Nazarkru, T.Den_Team. 2–3 – Snapic_PhotoProduction. 4–5 – blurAZ, Gorodenkoff. 6–7 – Onjira Leibe, FamVeld, Oxy_gen. 8–9 – MagicBones, Asia Images, Ryjkov_S, Sabelskaya, William Perugini, alazur, mei yanotai, Walter Cicchetti. 10–11 – T.W. van Urk, trezordia, Drazen Zigic. 12–13 – Peter Titmuss, Dzianis_Rakhuba, Photographer253, Little Hand Creations, Mr. Luck, Hein Nouwens. 14–15 – l i g h t p o e t, bsd, Martyn Jandula, John And Penny, Yganko, NWM, Anatolir, Rvector. 16–17 – pisaphotography, joyfull, SB7, MicroOne, Kolonko. 18–19 – joyfull, SB7, MicroOne, Kolonko. 20–21 – vystekimages, AL Robinson, 1494. 22–23 – Littlekidmoment, CharacterFamily70, YummyBuum, Rvector.

CONTENTS

Words that look like **this** can be found in the glossary on page 24.

HERE TO HELP

There are lots of jobs in the world and each one is different. Some jobs are always needed. The people who do these jobs are called key workers.

Key can sometimes mean needed and important.

Ambulance drivers are always needed to take hurt people to the hospital.

Without key workers, we would not have the things we need to live safely, such as food and important **services**.

PEOPLE IN TRANSPORTATION

Have you ever been on a bus or traveled somewhere by train? **Public** transportation lets us travel to and from places, whether it is for work, school, or fun!

Lots of people work in transportation. They work hard to make sure there are ways to travel. Let's learn about different key workers who work in transportation!

ON THE ROAD

Taxis are a great way to get from one place to another. Taxi drivers drive taxis during the day and night. They usually know the fastest **routes** around the city or town they work in.

Bus drivers follow a set route. They are **trained** to drive big buses through busy cities and streets. They pick up **passengers** at bus stops.

A bus station is where lots of different buses pick up passengers. People who work at bus stations can help travelers find the right bus.

Buses need to be cleaned too! Lots of passengers travel on buses, so it is important they are kept clean and tidy. Bus cleaners make sure buses are clean for us.

ON THE RAILWAYS

Lots of people work to keep trains running. Ticket offices in train stations are run by assistants who can help you buy the right ticket. They also make sure everybody gets on the train in time.

Technicians make sure that the railway tracks work properly. They test the tracks and fix them if they are broken or not safe. They also keep the tracks clear.

Train conductors usually work on trains. They make sure that everyone has the correct ticket and make **announcements** to everyone on board.

Train control room

Trains are driven by train drivers. They make sure everybody arrives safely. A train controller works elsewhere in a center. They give train drivers signals and let them know about any problems.

UNDER THE GROUND

Some big cities have trains that run underground in large tunnels. The trains are driven by train drivers.

Passenger trains that go underground are also called subways.

Just like other railways, the underground railways need to be properly looked after. Engineers work hard to make sure the underground railway tracks work safely.

ON

WATER

A ferry is a boat that takes passengers across water, from one **dock** to another. A ferry captain drives the ferry.

A ferry crew runs things on the ferry. They look after passengers and make sure everything is running smoothly. Some ferries transport **cargo**. The ferry crew looks after the cargo.

REPAIRED AND READY

Without public transportation, some people wouldn't be able to go to school or work. It's important to make sure taxis, buses, trains, and ferries are working properly.

How do you get to school?

Mechanics are needed to keep public transportation running. They check vehicles and can fix them if they are broken.

SAFE TRAVELS

Many different people work hard to make sure we can get where we need to go. Always remember to say thank you if you take public transportation.

Now you know about some of the people who work in transportation! Can you match each job below to the right person?

Train conductor

Checks train tickets and makes announcements to train passengers

Bus driver

Picks up passengers from bus stops

Railway technician

Checks and fixes railway tracks

GLOSSARY

announcements	messages that are given to everyone, usually about important information
cargo	things that are being transported by a ship or plane
dock	a place where a ship can stay while things are put on board or taken off board, or while the ship is repaired
passengers	people who are carried in or on something that is moving
public	to do with everyone
routes	paths or ways that are planned out so something can get from one point to another
services	tasks or actions that people pay other people to do, such as caring for older people, fixing things that are broken, or cleaning
trained	having been taught how to do a job

INDEX